21 Conversations

by

Deidra Whitt Lovegren

To Maryanne Marks Hurtado—the best of all possible women, mothers, English teachers, and friends.

You never needed to govern yourself accordingly.

Preface

We get it.

We live in the age of archetypes, so why weigh down the conversation with ornate description? We're not in the 18th century. (Otherwise, we'd be in the Age of Enlightenment, and who has time for that?)

So talk to me.

Speak your heart, directly and succinctly and recklessly.

Make me cry.

Make me fall in love.

Make me feel something.

Make me question my life's choices up to this point.

Just leave out the unnecessary details.

So, c'mon.

Hold my hand.

Let's go together.

Contents

Honestly

"O Woman-That-I-Used-To-Love, what should we get for dinner tonight?"

"Honestly, my Greatest-Disappointment? I don't care."

"You do care. You want me to suggest a place to eat so you can shoot it down. Whatever I say, you will wrinkle your little nose like I decided that we should eat out of the cat's litter box."

"You could not be more wrong, but you usually are."

"Perhaps you could stop on the way home and pick up some takeout."

"I could, but I won't. Our nightly conversation about dinner is the only authentic communication we will have all day, so I'm going to stretch it out as long as possible. It's the only way I can exert control over you in an as passive-aggressive way as possible since I know you are hungry and short-tempered."

"All true. Hey, I'll order Pad Thai. Not that you are satisfied with anything, but you usually don't hate that. I won't order spring rolls because you like them. Instead, I'll get the crispy ones I like—just to piss you off. When you complain, I'll counter with the idea of you picking up dinner next time. Then you will sulk in the bedroom, and I can watch TV peacefully without you talking during the interesting parts."

"Eh, I don't really want Thai food."

"Of course not. What do you want?"

"I want you to treat me like you did when we were dating."

"I want you to look like you did when we were dating. How about Taco Bell?"

"How about someplace that doesn't have paper napkins or E. coli outbreaks?"

"How fancy do you want to get on a Wednesday? And why do you agonize over every meal like it's going to be your last? It's just food, not a commitment—like the one you roped me into. You weren't really pregnant, were you?"

"Of course not. But I thought I could have been."

"Ah, yes. We've never really talked about your duplicity at the beginning, but we'll just sweep that under the rug and not worry about it for another few years until we're forced into marriage counseling."

"Agreed. But for tonight, I want to sit down and order off a menu. I don't want to get takeout, drive-thru, fast casual, pick a number, or a microwave burrito at 7-11. Let's go to a restaurant with actual waiters and waitresses. You do remember waitresses? I believe the last affair you had was with the blonde waitress at the diner by your work."

"Hardly an affair. More like a two-month fling. She went back to college in the fall. So, how about we save sit-down restaurants for special occasions? Like the weekend? I can't remember eating out every night as a kid. My mother cooked three meals a day!"

"Your mother didn't have to work. If we could afford it, I'd like to sit home, stir a box of Rice-A-Roni, overcook pork chops, and dish out a side order of childhood trauma—just like your mother."

"You are nothing like my mother. Sometimes I wish I could conjure up enough emotion to hate you. As it is, you're an annoyance. A mosquito in the room. Hair on a bar of soap. Gum on my shoe."

"Applebees."

"Applebees?"

"Or some other mid-price family restaurant. Just pick one. Texas Roadhouse. Olive Garden. Outback Steakhouse."

"Perfect. We'll go to a full-service restaurant and get a $7.99 Molten Lava Chocolate Cake for you to take one bite out of. Then you can sit on your bottom while women half your age scurry around to bring you as many Diet Cokes as you wish— along with a platter of limes! In the entire 19th century, the British Navy consumed fewer limes than you do."

"I. Can't. Wait. Let's go to a restaurant where you will reject the first three seatings we are offered, embarrassing me in front of the waitstaff. What do you have against sitting in a booth, anyway? You will ask the waiter what's on draft, order Miller Lite regardless, and eat the entire bread basket. After looking at the menu for ten seconds, you will order the least healthy thing—stuffed, battered, buttered, fried, creamy, glazed, supersized, or chocolate-encrusted. And yes, you do want fries with that. A double order!"

"And you...after fifteen minutes of reading the menu like an Egyptologist seeing the Rosetta Stone for the first time, you will order what you always do: a grilled chicken breast. $17.99

for a bland slab of frozen chicken you could microwave at home.”

“You want me to cook at home? Gordon Ramsay couldn’t conjure up beans on toast on those ancient appliances.”

“Here we go.”

“You promised me we’d move into a larger house when the kids got bigger. Well, they got bigger and left for college. Now it’s just you and me in the same 2000-square-foot shack.”

“That shack is almost paid for. I’m sick of house hunting. There is no need to move. Why do you want to double our mortgage? Stop watching HGTV. If you’re lucky, maybe Joanna and Chip Gaines will feature our shack on Fixer Upper.”

“If only you were half the man Chip Gaines is.”

“If only you were half as good-looking as Joanna.”

“You don’t lift a finger to help around the house.”

“You haven’t lifted a pot or pan since the kids left for college. Why have appliances if you aren’t going to use them?”

“The same reason you have a gym membership.”

“Oh my god, I am not going to sit across any restaurant table and look at your face for forty-five minutes. I don’t want to hear you complain about who didn’t unjam the copier at work. I don’t want to hear about your father’s recent medical appointment and what was lanced. All I can stomach right now is making a decision about what we want to eat. I will buy it, see you shove it down your gullet, and pat myself on the back for not loading up the car and leaving you tonight.”

"Oh, please leave tonight. I will help you pack. I'll try not to miss the long evenings when you talk to the dog more than me, the clothes you can't quite get into the hamper, and the half dozen glasses you leave around the house for the dishwashing fairy."

"So, pizza?"

"Pizza's always good."

"Darling, what should we get for dinner tonight?"

"Honestly, babe? I don't care."

"So, pizza?"

"Pizza's always good."

Can't Get Enough of What You Don't Need

"Stop that. It's disgusting."

"Mom, it's not my fault. The dining hall serves only three types of food: fried, deep fried, and grease fire."

"How about eating more fruits and vegetables? Surely the university has a salad bar on campus. Eat something unprocessed once in a while. Try a banana or an orange."

"They'd just fry that, too."

"I'm not driving for the next four hours with you passing gas. Stop eating so much junk."

"No."

"Hand over the bag of Skittles."

"Fine."

"You can't get enough of what you don't need."

"You're eating them all!"

"I can. I'm old."

"You make a point."

"So, how are classes going?"

"Everyone in freshman math is freaking out since the professor supposedly busted people for using Chegg. What is cheating in the 21st century anyway? Aren't we in a collaborative learning structure? We, as a society, should work collectively to accomplish collective purposes."

"That's some elegant bullshit."

"Thank you."

"At some point, you are going to have to define what cheating means to you. Throughout my life, I've found that a cheat is a cheat is a cheat."

"That sounds reductive."

"There it is: reductive. I swear they must teach that word at freshman orientation so students can use it in everyday conversation. Debating politics is reductive. Religion is reductive."

"Fine, that sounds repetitive."

"My point is that people who cheat on school assignments will probably grow up to cheat on their job applications, their taxes, their spouses. Cutting corners leads to nowhere good."

"Right. We are all going to hell."

"There is no hell."

"Hell is other people."

"Stop farting."

"I'm hungry."

"We'll stop at the next exit."

"Dad said you're writing again."

"Well, there's time now that you're all gone. Empty nesting is good for encouraging one's hobbies, I suppose."

"Cool. Does Dad read your stuff?"

"Your dad reads The Bar Journal. I don't think he cares much for my musings when he can read about the limits of statutory authority for tax audit estimates."

"Hey, if you want to make money, write children's books."

"I don't want to make money."

"How easy would it be to write a children's book? Just pick an animal that everyone likes—like a panda. Give it an alliterative name: Peter Panda. Have it search for food: Peter Panda Finds a Pizza. Then work in numerals and colors: one brown pizza crust, two red scoops of sauce, three white mushrooms."

"I don't want to write children's books."

"You can make bank, Mom."

"How about I just write for myself?"

"I know! You should write a self-help book for college girls. Call it Conquering Your 20s: A Woman's Journey."

"Hard pass. Anyway, you have your demographics wrong. If I wrote a self-help book—and that's highly unlikely—it would be targeted at suburban women. For a title, I'd just pick three verbs. Ponder Accept Believe."

"You have to mention chocolate in the title."

"You are so right. How about Chocolate Prayers and Red Wine Blessings?"

"Sounds like a bestseller."

"Look, not that you want to hear this, but most middle-aged women just want raunchy romance novels."

"Gross."

"It's true. They want to curl up with a paperback novel with a spray-tanned, half-naked anabolic steroid user on the front. Preferably with long flowing hair. One who is aggressively embracing a reluctant maiden. A bodice ripper."

"What's a bodice?"

"It's a lace-up top. The girl on the cover needs to have long hair because it's all part of the fantasy. Women start losing their hair by the handfuls in their 40s, so they daydream about having long locks for some debauched duke to pull."

"You are saying that women have rape fantasies."

"I am telling my college-aged son that college-aged girls do NOT have rape fantasies. Are we clear on this?!"

"We are clear."

"Say it. Say college-aged girls do NOT have rape fantasies."

"College-aged girls do NOT have rape fantasies, but apparently their mothers do."

"Now who's being reductive?"

"Seriously, I don't get any of it, Mom. A good-looking guy flirts with a girl? That's romantic. If an ugly guy attempts to flirt? It's harassment. How does anyone negotiate sexual politics? How can you play any game when you don't know the rules? I don't want to be on the news for some miscommunication."

"Maybe Dad can draw up some consent forms for you to photocopy."

"It's not funny. I don't want to be accused of anything bad."

"I agree. It's not funny. But I assume you know that drunk

girls cannot consent, and I assume you treat your partners with respect."

"How do you meet someone decent? The girls who I'm attracted to can't carry on a conversation, and the ones who are smart and funny aren't appealing to me."

"Well, dear, you need to figure yourself out first. The Greeks carved Know thyself on the temple of Apollo for a reason. Shakespeare wrote: To thine own self be true. If you can figure yourself out, then you won't be false to any man. Or woman."

"But how do you find the one?"

"Who says there's just one?"

"You know what I mean. You and Dad. You seem to have it all figured out."

"Yep, we do. For the most part."

"I don't think I'll ever figure girls out."

"Look. Everyone you will meet has relationship advice to offer. Gather it, think about it, and figure out what works for you."

"Ponder Accept Believe?"

"Hah. Now here's my advice. If you want passion, date yourself. Find a girl who thinks and acts just like you."

"Okay."

"But passion burns hot and doesn't last long."

"What if I want it to last long?"

"Then you'd better find someone who complements your personality. Find the yin to your yang."

"Dualism."

"Right. Dualism."

"Good to know."

"A caveat, though. Dating your complement might strip the passion right out."

"So you are saying that since I'm bad with money, I should find a rich wife to pay the bills."

"I'm saying live your life and make your own mistakes."

"I will. And oops. My bad."

"Gah! Maybe schedule a colonoscopy before next semester. Try eating more fiber."

Sol's Sunshine

"You cannot hit Jeremiah Brown in the face."

"But Pop Pop, JB is the worst boy in the entire 2nd grade!"

"Sunshine, I don't care if he's the worst boy in the entire state of Tennessee. You are not the kind of girl who uses her fists to talk for her. I've taught you better than that."

"What am I supposed to do when JB tells everyone at recess that I smell like dog pee?"

"You do not smell like dog pee."

"Missus Thatcher thinks so, too. She said I should soak my clothes in baking soda and warm water for an hour. I tried it once, but all we had was baking powder, and that didn't do nothin'."

"You tell Missus Thatcher to mind her own business. That woman has enough skeletons in her closet to fill up a cemetery."

"Is she a witch?"

"Puh. Almost."

"JB says our dogs pee all over the house because there ain't no one home to clean it. That's why he says we stink."

"Our house is clean enough, and we do not stink. If you think we stink, then you know how to do the washing as well as I do."

"Sometimes I forget to put the detergent in, Pop Pop. That makes the dog pee smell worse."

"Water ain't no good without soap. You need to remember that."

"I can't remember everything all the time."

"You're going to have to remember lots of things, Sunshine. It's my job to teach you, but when I'm teaching you, you gotta open up both of your ears. When I'm done teaching you, you gotta close your ears so nothing leaks out."

"My ears get tired of listening."

"I understand because I get tired of teaching the same things to you over and over."

"I'm sorry."

"Oh, don't listen to me, Sunshine. I love talking to you, and it was foolish of me to say otherwise. People say foolish things all the time, so don't take none of it seriously. You know, if people didn't talk nonsense, then the world would be awfully quiet. Try to talk only when you have something to say."

"I'll try to remember that."

"You're going to have to remember lots of things as you grow up. You have to remember to bring your lunch and your backpack to school. Every single day."

"I'm trying."

"I can't keep taking time off work every time you forget your show-and-tell project or lose your house key or punch some no-account boy."

"JB can count. He might be mean, but he's good at math. I

copy off his paper sometimes."

"You just leave that boy be. I know his whole family. Nothing good has come from that family for four generations."

"I forgot to tell you. The school is selling generations for Easter. Can we get one?"

"Do you mean geraniums or carnations?"

"Maybe both. I can't remember."

"Your Grandma always said that a child who always forgets has a mother who always remembers."

"Well, I don't have either. I don't have a mom, and I don't have a grandma."

"Yes, you do. I've shown you their pictures…"

"Pictures don't tell nobody nothin'."

"I told you stories about them, too."

"Like what?"

"Like how your mother liked vanilla ice cream cones with sprinkles on top. Like how your grandmother made your pink-and-purple checkered quilt—just before you were born."

"What other stories do you know?"

"Well, how we decided to name you Heidi after your grandmother. But did you know Heidi was her favorite book as a child? I have a copy on the bookshelf in your room. When you get older, we'll read it together."

"No one calls me Heidi, and no one calls you Solomon. You're Sol and I'm Sunshine."

"That's because the moment you were born, you screamed and

hollered like a scalded cat. It was only when I sang 'You are my sunshine, my only sunshine' did you quiet down a little."

"Why did I cry so much as a baby?"

"You were very sick."

"Did I have chicken pox?

"No, Sunshine."

"What was wrong with me then?"

"You were going through withdrawal."

"What's that?"

"It's hard to explain. You see, your mother liked to take something that she thought made her feel better, but it ended up making her very sick."

"How sick?"

"So sick that she had to go to a special place to live. So sick that she can never take care of you. So God gave you to me and Grandma to raise."

"Then why did Grandma die before I was born?"

"I ask Him the same question every night. I don't know. It's a paradox."

"A pair of ducks?"

"No, no. A paradox is a mystery. Something that doesn't make sense until you look at it just the right way."

"Like JB."

"What do you mean, like JB?"

"I hit him because I like him. It don't make any sense."

"Oh, that makes all the sense in the world. It's the people we love who make us the maddest. Then when they're gone, we miss them like crazy."

"Do you miss Grandma?"

"I keep forgetting she's gone. I talk to her like she's sitting right next to me in the car."

"Pop Pop, I'm sitting next to you in the car, not Grandma."

"It's easy to make that mistake. You look just like her. You look like your mom, too."

"Do you miss my mom?"

"I missed the little girl your mom used to be. I'll tell you what. Let's go over to the Dairy Queen and get some vanilla ice cream cones."

"With sprinkles."

"With extra sprinkles. You can tell me about JB and how you'll never punch him or another boy again."

"Are you still mad at me?"

"There's no getting mad at you. You are my Sunshine, my only sunshine, and I love you. Don't you ever forget that."

"Oh, Pop Pop, that's the easiest thing in the world to remember."

The 10th Circle of Hell

"Virgil?"

"Yes, Dante."

"Um, what's going on here? I was told there were only nine circles of hell."

"There were only nine circles of hell in the 20th century. But for the 21st century? We needed to expand."

"You needed to expand...hell."

"Yes. We've added a whole new circle. Well, truthfully, it's more oblong than circular. It's been that sort of millennium."

"Virgil. In all seriousness, I'm not sure I can walk through another realm of the damned. It's hella depressing."

"Well, you don't have much of a choice, do you? You read the sign: Abandon all hope, ye who enter here. Did that sound like a joke to you?"

"No."

"Then maybe you should remember why you are here."

"Yes. Beatrice! Beatrice!"

"Exactly. Beatrice, the love of your life—whom you've seen exactly twice. That seems a little on the obsessive side, don't you think? Yet, it is true. Beatrice is waiting for you in paradise."

"Oh my lady love, wait for me! Lead on, Virgil. Take me to

paradise to see my dearest once more! Third time's the charm."

"If you insist."

"Of course, I insist. And are you getting snarky with me?"

"Who, me?"

"Yes, Virgil. What's your problem?"

"You want to see Beatrice. Great, I get that. But how about your own wife, Dante? Would you like to see her, too?"

"Leave Gemma out of this."

"Just so you know, Gemma Donati has an apartment just down the cloud from Beatrice. You can see both of your lady friends when we get to paradise, I suppose."

"Virgil—"

"And I guess that arranged marriage didn't work out as well as your parents planned? They're in paradise, too. You can ask your mom when you see her who she likes better."

"Virgil—"

"That's assuming you even make it to paradise. Seriously, with your slinky link? You're lucky you didn't end up in a second circle of hell whirlwind with the rest of the lotharios. And Helen of Troy."

"Virgil, I don't need your judgment."

"I know you don't need my judgment. That's what we have King Minos for."

"Ugh, I hate that guy."

"You hate the king of Hell proper—the place where nothing gleams? Dante, it's hell. It's not Disney World."

"Have you been on It's a Small World? There are similarities."

"Dante."

"C'mon, Virgil. You have to admit that a justice system dependent on a serpentine man wrapping his tail around dead human carcasses a corresponding number of times to assign them their circles of hell seems a little—subjective."

"It's worked for thousands of years. You know what we say in Rome, if it ain't broke—"

"Conquer it?"

"Ha. Colonizer humor. I like it."

"Just take me to Beatrice. I don't care how long it takes! I love her!"

"Sure, Dante. I'm sure you do."

"You wouldn't understand."

"Dude, I'm Rome's greatest poet. I understand everything."

"Let's just keep going. Please."

"We have just a few more stops to make before then, Dante. There's the rest of hell to go through, and then purgatory…"

"ARE YOU SERIOUS."

"Yes, I'm serious. Stop pouting like a little bitch or I'll take you back to the 5th circle of hell where you belong, Mr. Sullen."

"Sullen? I'm not sullen. I'm upset."

"Wrathful. Sullen. Disappointed. Upset. All the same circle of hell, fella. Numero Cinco."

"Ugh. I'm exhausted! This is a lot of walking, spiraling down into one horror show after another. I get it. Hell sucks. When are we getting to purgatory? I mean, aren't you tired?"

"I'm a ghost, Dante. We don't get tired. We just get annoyed."

"Ugh. I hate this place! It smells like sulfur, burnt hair, llama breath, and ass."

"Well, it is hell, Dante. The netherworld. The Inferno. Gehenna, Tophet, Abaddon. Sheol, Hades, Tartarus…"

"A T.J. Maxx dressing room on a Saturday afternoon. A Tinder date. A middle school classroom right after lunch just before holiday break. Wet woolen socks. An M. Night Shyamalan movie."

"Yep. All hellscapes."

"Can we just leave?"

"No, we can't just leave. The love of your life, Beatrice, sent me to drag your sorry ass through all of hell and purgatory."

"Beatrice, I'm coming!"

"Seriously, man. Maybe rethink your attachment disorders."

"You will love Beatrice, Virgil. Just one look and you will write another epic poem—one as great as the Aeneid!"

"I wrote about the founding of Rome, not the founding of your overtaxed libido. Give it a rest. Besides, I'll never meet her."

"Why not?"

"You know the rules, Dante. Everyone born before the birth of our lord and savior gets tossed into limbo. No baptism? No passing Go. No collecting $200. Virtuous pagans, all."

"Even Moses? Abraham?"

"Yep. Even Julius Fricking Caesar."

"Look, I saw the first circle of hell. It isn't that bad, is it?"

"It's a Starbucks with a broken espresso machine."

"So, where are we now?"

"Let me get the map. Hmm."

"Do we have to cross any more icky rivers?"

"Not really, but the Acheron, Styx, and Phlegethon all freeze together into a cesspool in the ninth circle."

"Lake Cocytus?"

"Exactly."

"Some politicians I know have a summer home there."

"Actually, that's a requirement when they sell their soul. But it's more of a timeshare arrangement, to be honest. Not the best investment, but illiquid assets usually aren't."

"I think we are here."

"Nope. We're done with the eighth circle. What a shitshow that place is."

"Who knew fraud came in so many flavors?"

"Well, we have ten evil ditches to sort them all into...It's awfully hard to tell a hypocrite from a panderer from a United States Congressman."

"That's a lot of blue suits and flag pins!"

"The bigger the flag pin, the bigger the crook."

"All right. So we've been through limbo, lust, gluttony, greed, anger, heresy, violence, fraud, and treachery. That seems like it should cover everything. So what's the new tenth circle of hell?"

"You know. How could you not know?"

"I can't fathom what is worse than all of those other sins and evils of mankind."

"TikTok. TikTok is the tenth circle of hell."

"That seems fair."

L'odeur of Summer 1794

"Find us a good place to sit, Suzanne. In front of the scaffold, but not too close."

"Absolument. I know just the spot."

"I will be back shortly."

"Where are you going, Jacqueline?"

"To buy a nosegay."

"Who's selling flowers on such a day?"

"There's a stall near the tumbrels—next to the prisoner carts. The lilacs have bloomed."

"Lilacs!"

"Oui, lilacs. Why not lilacs? They'll match my dress."

"Mon Dieu! Are you sprucing up for the gendarme?"

"Would you fault me for it? John-Paul is tall, strapping—like my Raphaël was."

"John-Paul is an excellent national guardsman. He proved himself yesterday when the executioner needed a strong hand. How the marquis slipped the blocks before the blade fell is a mystery."

"Only to make a botch of the whole thing. The blade took off the left side of his face—down to the shoulder."

"Heh heh. Imagine having your head blocked in twice—set like a common criminal in the stocks. John-Paul had to hold down the marquis like a farm animal. Embarrassant!"

"Agreed. So who is the executioner?"

"Charles-Henri Sanson."

"Sanson is good. He will keep the line moving quickly."

"John-Paul will keep your heart beating quickly."

"I tell you, Suzanne. If I weren't already a step into the grave, I'd let John-Paul hold me down. I'd show him a good time."

"Oh, go on. You are a tricoteuse, not a courtesan! You hold knitting needles in your hands, not silk gloves."

"I am not the ugliest crone in the crowd."

"In truth, Jacqueline, you still have vestiges of beauty. But what did your good looks ever earn you on the estates?"

"Young lords."

"And their fathers…"

"The young lords were good for a tumble, but the old lords were good for a trinket. Dieu merci, I am glad those days are over. Being an old woman brings peace."

"With the aristos gone, our days of peace are ahead, so to speak. Ha Hah! Liberté, égalité, fraternité!"

"I keep hoping to see the aristos I've known over the years waiting in the carts. Especially the ones with the cruel wives."

"Their Day of Judgment is here, thanks to Robespierre."

"Ah, look. The crowd is even larger. I will buy flowers before the sun grows too hot, before the Place de la Révolution smells like a slaughterhouse."

"Too late—there are the priests. They've begun to read the psalms, Jacqueline. Come knit with me, and we'll keep track of the heads. No time left for lilacs, the carts, or dreams of John-Paul."

"Can't a woman dream between knits and purls?"

"Young women can dream, Jacqueline."

"True, Suzanne. Old women mainly have nightmares."

"Look! They line up. I wonder who will feed la guillotine? Did you recognize anyone in the tumbrels?"

"Non, but I do not like to see them beforehand—the rich and powerful—covered in their own filth. Duc, marquis, comte, vicomte, baron—trussed up like Christmas geese."

"You pity them in such a state?"

"I trust Robespierre, and Robespierre pities no enemy of the Republic. He and the Committee of Public Safety will save France from counter-revolutionaries."

"Ah, what a line to the scaffold! La guillotine is especially hungry."

"Much quicker than hanging or the ax. Now those were true spectacles d'horreur."

"Sauvage et inhumain."

"It's good for people in power to see the people's power. Robespierre knows what he's doing."

"By killing off his political rivals?"

"You doubt him?"

"I doubt everything."

"Even God?"

"Especially God."

"Don't blaspheme, Suzanne. Sit! They begin. Can you hear the aristo's final words?"

"Not quite. Something about 'pardoning those who have occasioned my death.' Je m'emmerde! I am so bored. You'd think aristos would say something more memorable at their end."

"Oof—the blade is swift."

"The next one is already in the cabbage! How quickly they are proceeding. Remember last week when the blade dulled?"

"The blade was sharp enough. It caught on the fat necks of the aristos. Some are so corpulent la guillotine's blade must come down on it again and again."

"Imagine having so much to eat."

"Chop chop chop! The executioner is swift. One every minute. Hold the head up high, Executioner! Yes, yes! Higher!"

"Ha Hah! That's a grisly piece of business."

"It's hard to look down your nose, Mr. Aristo, when there is nothing below it to see!"

"The basket is already getting full, and the heads are getting ripe. L'odeur!"

"How you complain! You know how these things go, Suzanne."

"Still, the stench."

"Cover your nose and mouth with your scarf. Perhaps I should have gotten my lilacs after all. How many rivers of blood and pools of merde have we seen this past year?"

"I won't have my dress splattered like last time!"

"An easy fix. Just soak your frock in cold water with white vinegar."

"I know. I know. When I used to be a laundress, I knew all the tricks. Soda ash cleaned the blood from my clothes when my vicomtesse whipped me to shreds."

"Now, your vicomtesse is a pile of ash!"

"Ha Hah! That she is."

"Robespierre sent them to the scaffold last winter. It was a good day. Bright and clear."

"Look at this, Jacqueline! I've finished another one."

"Let me see. Oui, you knit so well. Your latest liberty cap! Let me wear it while you start another."

"I am almost out of red yarn."

"I brought along another spool in my bag. I knew today would be long. So much commotion in Paris."

"La guillotine is on number nine."

"Already?"

"Who is next?"

"That's Antoine Simon—a friend of Robespierre. He guards the dauphin. I don't understand why he is on the scaffold."

"He won't be for long. So quick! Look at the head. Are you sure that is Simon?"

"Oui. He belonged to the Commune of Paris. He must have been a spy."

"Or a counter-revolutionary."

"Bien sûr. Robespierre is masterful at finding wolves in sheep's clothing."

"Who's next in line?"

"Hard to tell. The man's face is so swollen—wrapped tight—the jaw bleeds…"

"He stands so still."

"See how regal he is. How stoic! He walks the steps as if he knows them well."

"His bandages will have to be removed to prepare the neck."

"Oh, that cry. That man's jaw is shattered. It's in pieces!"

"La guillotine will stop his shrieks—end his pain."

"The blade drops! Finally, finally."

"The crowd cheers at that one. Who was he? Can you see?"

"Non-non-non—ça ne peut pas être!"

"Jacqueline, qu'est-ce? Whose head is that?

"Sacré bleu! None other than Robespierre."

"Then who will lead us now?"

"Chaos."

Florida Man

Miami

"Well, that was dramatic."

"You know the drill. We had to put a hood on you. It's better if you don't know where you are."

"You could have just beaten me up on the street."

"Where's the fun in that? Now look, Ricky, we're tired of waiting for our money."

"I got your money—it's just tied up."

"No, you are tied up. Hit him again."

"That's not necessary. Oof!"

"C'mon, Ricky. Don't make us mess up your pretty face. Well, maybe it's not so pretty anymore, and maybe your girlfriend won't like you as much anymore."

"Keep my girlfriend's name out of your mouth."

"Don't you worry about my mouth. You need to worry about your own and if you'll leave here with any teeth left. But I'm sure you can find yourself a good dentist in Magic City."

"You know, I've always wanted veneers."

"Hit him again."

"No, wait! Oof. That's a crown! You know how expensive crowns are to replace?"

"Miguel will take out your front teeth next. Both in one jab. Pop!"

"I'm sure he could, and I'll get your money. Are we done here?"

"You know, Ricky, you look a little bloated. Maybe too much inflammation. My wife has me taking turmeric or some yellow powdery shit to stop inflammation. Swelling is apparently the root of all the evils for men my age. Of course, my girlfriend has me taking Cialis, but that's a whole other story."

"That's a whole other swelling problem."

"Funny guy. I should get Miguel to hit you again, but I'm going to steal your joke."

"Tell you what. I'll give you the joke. Let's just call it even."

"Just get the money and bring it to Pensacola. You have a week."

Orlando

"How do I look, Ricky?"

"Like a sexy, overworked Disney employee. Where'd you get these uniforms?"

"Goodwill. They have loads of them."

"And name badges? Why are we both CHRIS from Orlando?"

"It's the default ID badge for Disney Cast Members when they forget to wear their own. Ricky, there wasn't a lot of choice on eBay. I did the best I could."

"You did great."

"I did really great. I even managed to extract two blue employee passes, so we can get through the cheese graters."

"You rummage through some employees' cars?"

"Didn't need to. Just good ol' fashioned pickpocketing."

"Honey, we're not going to have a lot of time."

"Tell me the plan again."

"We park near the employee exit, walk to the employee entrance, find our way to the Okapi enclosure, then take the baby."

"What's a baby Okapi weigh?"

"Like 35 pounds or something. It's like a big toddler."

"A toddler that looks like a cross between a zebra and a giraffe. How much are we getting for this kidnapping, anyway?"

"It's not a kidnapping. It's an animal exchange program, where we exchange a baby cud-chewing hoofed mammal for a crazy old man's money."

"Oh, that sounds much better."

"There is no way this plan is going to work."

"Exactly. It's so incredibly stupid. It's perfect."

"You ready, CHRIS from Orlando?"

"I'm ready, CHRIS from Orlando."

The Villages

"Oh, look at this bee-yoo-ti-ful creature. God had fun making this little guy (cough)."

"Thank you. My wife and I knew he would find a good home with you and your—uh, menagerie. You have quite a collection."

"I must say I am very pleased (cough). Now, what was our agreement?"

"$10,000 upon delivery. Plus expenses."

"Good, good. I usually keep that amount or so in the cookie jar here (cough). You want a cookie? There's some Lorna Doone on the counter."

"No thanks, we actually need to be on our way."

"You can't stay? You'd like the Villages. We can rent you a golf cart to get around. It's karaoke and trivia night at Katie Belle's residence club. I can get you in."

"That sounds fantastic, but we're expected in Tallahassee for the FSU game."

"I understand. Sort of. I'm a Gator, so I can't stomach the sight of you 'Noles very much (cough)."

"Are you keeping the Okapi in a stable somewhere?"

"No, no (cough cough). We'll just let him run around the condo here (cough). I'm sure I can get a leash and take him out on a few walks. I have some lady friends who might walk him for me. Heh heh (cough cough cough)."

"Beg your pardon—but you're keeping the Okapi in your apartment?"

"It's a three-bedroom condo on the golf course. Plenty of room (cough). And he can graze on the 9th hole. There's a bugger of a sand trap nearby, but, you know, if the Okapi can survive the Congo—"

"Then he can certainly survive central Florida. Looks like you've thought this through."

"Son of a bitch (cough). The little bastard just took a dump on the parquet floor—you gonna clean that up?"

"I'm afraid, sir, our business transaction is complete. I hope you and your Okapi and your girlfriends all find joy in this lovely home."

Tallahassee

🏖🏖🏖

"I hate Tallahassee, Ricky."

"It's not that bad. The beer is cheap—and free-if you want to hit a frat party or two."

"We're about ten years too old for that. Let's keep going west to Pensacola. I love the sugar-white beaches, and you can pay off your debt."

"We will probably spend the night here once I cash out."

"Here? Even shitty hotels here are $350 a night—they jack the rates for every damn football game. All the restaurants are packed with crazed alumni. Everybody is half-naked and half-drunk. I hate it here, Ricky. Let's just go."

"I need to meet a guy."

"Ricky, you don't need to meet a guy. You don't need to bet on the FSU game. We have enough!"

"Honey, I'm doing a three-team parlay. The payout is at +300 or +400."

"Ricky, I have no idea what that means."

"Trust me?"

"Never."

"Good girl."

Pensacola

"Now what, Ricky? We don't even have money for coffee."

"Dine and dash?"

"I can't run in sandals. You should have told me your parlay went tits up last night, and I would have worn my running shoes. Or we could have done a little light shoplifting. The city is always in chaos for an hour or two after the game."

"Honey, you wanted a steak, and I wanted to buy you one."

"A legitimate meal. And the tip you left was substantial."

"I thought the girl earned it."

"You're being reckless."

"I have a plan."

"Uh oh. I know that look."

"It's Sunday."

"We're going to rob a megachurch, aren't we?"

"Render unto Caesar the things that are Caesar's, and unto God the things that are God's."

U.S. Army Issue Brown T-Shirt

"You can't keep me here."

"Please, Mr. Van de Kamp. Take your seat."

"You can't keep me here—"

"I assure you, we can. Your father—"

"My father can eat shit and die."

"Mr. Van de Kamp, such language will not be tolerated here. You are well aware of our Code of Conduct."

"Headmaster, you are well aware of my Code of Con-dick."

"Mr. Van de Kamp! Govern yourself accordingly. Please sit down. Have you checked into your dormitory this afternoon?"

"Have you checked into your wife because I hear she's pretty hot."

"Young man, I never—"

"Maybe that's the problem. The sexual revolution is going on—free love! Maybe your wife is on the pill. Maybe she is having the time of her life."

"Mr. Van de Kamp, I know you and your generation think you know everything. But as of today, September 5, 1967, you are still enrolled at this institution. Your father has signed the in loco parentis agreement. This school is legally responsible for you."

"Then this school—and you—can both eat shit and die."

"Mr. Van de Kamp!"

"Sir?"

"Your insolence is intolerable."

"Sir, yes sir. By the way, there's nothing you can do that can't be done…"

"Please sit up straight in your chair like a young man, not a barbarian."

"Nothing you can sing that can't be sung…"

"Mr. Van de Kamp, what is going to transpire now is—"

"Transpire. Transpire?"

"Transpire. Occur. To come about—"

"You-are-going-to-what?"

"I'm going to come about—"

"Pervert. All you boarding school types are perverts. I'm going to come about. Gross. No wonder your wife hates you."

"Mr. Van de Kamp, you are putting words in my mouth."

"What did you want me to put in your mouth?"

"Young man!"

"Nothing you can say, but you can learn how to play the game. It's easy."

"You are going to go back to your dormitory and dress appropriately for the dining hall. You must wear your school jacket and polo shirt when on the premises."

"I'm wearing this under my polo. One U.S. Army issue brown

t-shirt. It was my brothers."

"Headmaster? I'm dropping out of school next Wednesday when I turn 17."

"My mother—my MOTHER—is divorcing my father. She will sign the necessary forms."

"When I get out of here, I will head to Fort Dix. Eight weeks of basic training! If there are no SNAFUs, then I will fly to Fort Lewis before shipping out to Vietnam. Maybe I'll visit a prostitute near the base to lose my virginity. Or maybe not. It doesn't matter."

"I'm thinking they'll assign me to infantry. I'm ground troop material. Chum for the sharks. The Vietnamese call sharks cá mập. I've been studying their language, you lỗ đít."

"Oh, I mean to. And who knows? By Thanksgiving, I may be in the Tây Ninh Province on Nui Ba Den. Black Virgin Mountain. Exotic, no?"

"Nothing you can m-make that can't be made. No one you can save that can't be s-saved..."

"I've been practicing, you know. All summer. I can carry 60

pounds of gear. I know the military alphabet: alpha, beta, charlie. Charlie.”

“Maybe I’ll be a radio operator like—like my brother was. I—I could be a machine gunner. Or maybe a tunnel rat.”

“I’m not afraid of going over there. I know the language—I know some of it.”

“I think I ripped my polo shirt.”

Male #18

"It sounds like hell."

"You'll be fine."

"How does it work?"

"The women stay stationary in the circle while the men rotate around the perimeter. You'll switch to a new partner every three minutes."

"It sounds like square dancing. Do I allemande right or left?"

"You can't promenade with anyone unless you talk to someone. Be nice. Don't be an ass."

"When can we leave?"

"Let's go around the circuit at least once. The women fill out little cards about you and drop them off with the hostess."

"Perfect! I can be humiliated in real-time."

"That's the spirit."

"I'm not really up for this."

"Look, here are our name tags. See? You are lucky MALE #18."

"How is 18 lucky?"

"You are obviously not Jewish."

"If I were Jewish, I would be much more interesting."

"18. Chai. The Hebrew letters in chai add up to 18. It means alive and kicking. Rejoice! You're living."

"If you say so."

"Let's get you a drink. They're just about to start."

"Okay."

"You're Male #18. I'm Male #19. I'll warm up the ladies for you as you come around."

"Let's just let things proceed organically."

"Hi, I'm Male #18."

"I'm Female #18. We start with the same number until we rotate."

"Gotcha."

"So, what do you do?"

"How do I do?"

"No, I mean what. What is it that you do?"

"What do I do? Well, tonight, I am speed dating."

"First time?"

"Can you tell?"

"I can always tell."

"Have you done this before?"

"Yeah, a few times."

"Do you work nearby?"

"Yes, I work nearby. Um, Look. Let me guess. Recently

divorced, right?"

"No, it's been half a year."

"It's been six months. And trust me, you aren't over her. If you want my advice, just wait until you don't hate her anymore. The opposite of love is indifference. It's obvious you aren't ready to move on. Take care of yourself."

"Hi, I'm Male #18."

"God bless you."

"Sorry?"

"God bless you."

"Um—and also with you?"

"There are no accidents."

"How about car accidents? I don't think people smash into each other on purpose, right?"

"Everything happens for a reason."

"But reasonable people don't cause accidents."

"Hatred stirreth up strifes: but love covereth all sins."

"Hi Female #20. I'm Male #18."

"Hi Male #18. I hate all of my idiotic friends for dragging me here. The last guy asked me my bra size."

"Male #19? I'm sorry to say that he's my idiotic friend. I apologize for him."

"Why are you here?"

"Well, my life turned upside down six months ago, and I'm not even sure who I am anymore."

"Oh, rejection? I am an expert in the field. I majored in rejection in college."

"So, did you reject the Ramada Inn's nacho bar? That cheese-from-a-can looks delicious."

"Is there any chance you want to skip the other speed dating rounds? There is an excellent diner around the corner. It serves the best coconut cream pie you've ever had."

"You sure you don't want to talk to some other guys? Maybe Mr. Right is Male #17?"

Pink Martini

"I don't think I'm ready."

"You're ready. Besides, you don't have a choice."

"I don't have a chance."

"C'mon. She's sweet."

"She's scary."

"She's sweet and scary and—six years old. Look, I think you have a distinct advantage, being a grown up and all."

"Ugh...tell me what she wants to do again?"

"She wants to have tea with her mommy's new boyfriend."

"Where?"

"In the treehouse."

"Do I have to climb the tree?"

"Yes, you have to climb the tree—in your suit."

"Why do I have to wear a suit? I don't even wear a suit to work."

"She wants a formal tea party alone with you in the treehouse. Besides, you look so handsome in a suit and tie."

"Suit and tie?!"

"Of course. It's formal."

"Like a funeral."

"It'll be fun. I really like your navy suit—and please wear your pink tie. She really likes pink."

"If you had told me when we first started dating that treehouses and ties would be involved—"

"Nothing would have changed because you adore me. You are crazy about me. You love me."

"I do love you."

"And I love you, too. But it's time—past time—for you to meet my daughter. So meet my daughter."

"In a treehouse."

"For a cup of tea. Or most likely a juice box."

"I don't like the grape ones."

"How about apple?"

"Apple is good. I can live with apple."

"Go back to your apartment and get changed. Don't keep her waiting."

"All right, I'll go."

🐻🐻🐻

"What's in the teapot?"

"Tea."

"It looks purple."

"It's purple tea."

"Do you have snacks?"

"Yes."

"What kind of snacks?"

"I have pink sparkly cookies. Do you want one?"

"Yes, thank you. I'll take two. They look pink and delicious—and omigod—are these made of Play-Doh?"

"You aren't supposed to eat them."

"I thought they were real—do you have any napkins up here?"

"No. Just swallow them. Mom gets mad when I spit."

"Oh."

"I can pour you some tea if you want."

"That's grape juice."

"It's in a teacup. So it's tea."

"I was promised apple juice."

"I don't have any apple juice boxes. Grape is better anyway. Ooh. Sorry."

"Juice boxes squirt when you squeeze them too hard."

"I'm really sorry. Now your tie is pink and purple."

"I think it looks better this way."

"You aren't mad?"

"Not yet."

"Why do you have a hole in your pants?"

"Because whoever built this treehouse didn't hammer in the nails properly—and they should have used 10-inch long, ¾-inch diameter galvanized lag screws and washers."

"My dad built this treehouse."

"It's big."

"He doesn't live with us anymore."

"Your mother told me."

"Are you going to live here?"

"Not today."

"Tomorrow?"

"Ask me tomorrow."

"Do you want some more tea?"

"Of course—and you are right. The grape tastes better."

"I told you."

"Look at all this cool stuff. Coloring books. A sleeping bag. A few lizards to keep you company. You must have a lot of fun up here."

"I do."

"Does your mom ever come up?"

"No, she says it's my place."

"Well, thanks for inviting me."

"You want some more tea?"

"Sure."

"We could get some real cookies."

"We could. Hey, I brought you something."

"Can I open it?"

"Sure."

"It's a mirror!"

"It's a pink mirror...and we can hang it right—here."

"Okay."

"Are you ready to go in?"

"I don't think I'm ready."

"We better go. Your mom and I ordered pizza. I guess we could get it delivered to the treehouse next time. Pizza and tea?"

"I think I'd rather have a Coke."

"Your mom just texted. The pizza's here. Don't keep her waiting."

"All right, I'll go."

🍹 🍹 🍹

"What's in bubble tea?"

"You haven't ever had boba tea? Jeez, you are so lame."

"Seriously, look at this straw! It's big enough to suck up a meatball."

"Just drink it, and don't embarrass me."

"Is this candy at the bottom? Skittles? Jelly beans?"

"It's tapioca or something."

"Why are these little balls pink?"

"They're pretty and taste like strawberries."

"They taste like diabetes. I feel like I'm going to choke on this stuff. Do you know CPR?"

"Not really. They tried to teach us in P.E., but the boys were being disgusting with the CPR dummies."

"Just pound on my chest."

"I could probably keep you alive until the paramedics arrive."

"That would be helpful."

"You're welcome."

"So...we need to talk."

"What."

"I'm going to ask your mom to marry me."

"It's about time."

"You're okay with that?"

"Yeah, I'm okay with that."

"How do you think I should ask her?"

"You realize I'm thirteen. This is not really my skill set."

"Yeah, but you and your mom are close. You must have some advice."

"Just be yourself."

"I'm boring."

"You are definitely boring, but that is something she really likes about you."

"So, what's the boring way to ask someone to get married?"

"Fancy dinner. Get down on one knee. Open a little pink box. She'll cry. Everyone in the restaurant will clap."

"Okay."

"And I really like your navy suit—and please wear your pink tie."

"I threw that out years ago."

"Are you ready to go?"

"I don't think I'm ready. I want to finish this weird candy drink and buy a new tie."

"Mom's here to pick us up. Don't keep her waiting."

"All right, I'll go."

"What's in a pink martini?"

"Just drink it. Don't be such an old man."

"I am an old man. Can I just have a beer?"

"No. This is my special day, and you have to drink what I say."

"This tastes like pink sparkly Play-Doh."

"Oh, you are impossible! Just sip it. It's vodka, vermouth, orange bitters and grenadine."

"That is the exact recipe for pink sparkly Play-Doh. Mmm. Delicious. The pink martini is all gone now. Are you ready to go?"

"I don't think I'm ready."

"You're ready. Besides, you don't have a choice. Your groom awaits. How did someone as feisty as you meet such a good guy anyway?"

"It runs in the family."

"Hey—you hear that? That organ music is your cue to get

moving. Don't keep him waiting."

"All right, I'll go."

Madness Among the Flowers

"Thanks for coming after school, Sophie."

"I need to get my grades up."

"Well, I'm here to help. Let's go over some of the discussion questions."

"Okay."

"So what do you do when your values clash with society's?"

"I don't know."

"Think about it. You have a different worldview, different ethics, different principles. Your particular morality doesn't align with the status quo. So what do you do?"

"I don't know. This is why I'm failing English."

"Hamlet is challenging, but give him a chance. At this point in the play, he has three options."

"He could, like...move?"

"It's hard to move when you are the Prince of Denmark."

"He could kill himself."

"True. That is an option. It's not a great option, but Hamlet does consider suicide in several of his seven soliloquies."

"He could go crazy."

"Hamlet tries that. Or he pretends to be insane. Or he really is. Like most things in Hamlet and in life, the line between sanity and madness is paper thin."

"He could just laugh it off. I mean, life sucks."

"It definitely sucks at times, but you make a good point. Developing an exquisite sense of humor to cope with the absurdities of life is a viable option. Absurdism is more fun than nihilism."

"Hey, can I talk to you?"

"We are talking."

"I mean really talk to you."

"Of course."

"T-Thank you."

"What's going on, Sophie? Is this about the test you failed?"

"I failed another test."

"Math?"

"No. I failed a pregnancy test."

"Oh."

"I'm not sure what to do."

"You'll have to talk to your parents."

"They'll kill me!"

"They won't."

"I can't talk to my parents."

"You could talk to your guidance counselor. They can explain all of your options."

"I want the baby. We're Catholic."

"Then keep the baby. But you'll need assistance."

"My parents will be so embarrassed. I don't want to be a d-disappointment."

"Let me tell you about someone else who didn't want to be a disappointment."

"Who? Was Jenny Ostenkowski talking about me in class? I hate her."

"Don't worry about Jenny Ostenkowski. No one listens to her anyway. I want to tell you about Hamlet's girlfriend. Ophelia."

"Hamlet's girlfriend? I don't really know the play. I haven't really been listening…"

"No one pays attention to Hamlet until they need it. All of life's answers are contained in that one little play."

"Didn't you say it was Shakespeare's longest play? It's really long, Miss."

"It is long, but it's worth it."

"Okay."

"Ophelia is in the same situation as you. But instead of the Lehnhart boy, Hamlet is the jerk in question."

"Asshole is more like it."

"Because Ophelia is lower class, she cannot speak her mind to Hamlet's parents. So she says what she needs to with flowers."

"How?"

"Flowers have meanings. Clear, unequivocal meanings."

"Like r-red roses for true love?"

"Exactly. First, Ophelia gives her brother rosemary and pansies. This represents remembrance and faithfulness. She wants her brother to find their father's killer. That should be his priority. Just like the Lehnhart boy should be making you and his child his priority."

"Exactly! Jack Lehnhart ghosted me when I told him."

"Like Hamlet, the Lehnhart boy may not marry you, but he needs to face up to his responsibility."

"I know, right?"

"Next, Ophelia gives the king fennel and columbines. Fennel represents flattery, and columbines symbolize foolish adultery, especially in men. Ophelia was brave. She insulted the king to his face!"

"Just using flowers? What a badass."

"Ophelia was a badass. Especially when she handed the queen a bouquet of rue, saying, 'There's rue for you, and here's some for me. O, you must wear your rue with a difference.' She was basically calling Hamlet's mother a slut for marrying his uncle as soon as Hamlet's father died."

"No way."

"And rue was used to induce abortions 400 years ago. So what does that say about our cheating Queen?"

"She's a thot."

"Then, Ophelia holds up some daisies in front of the entire court and gives them to nobody! Daisies mean innocence. She called everyone out."

"Shut. Up. That is so cool."

"Finally, with sweet violets, she approaches the king and queen and says, 'I would give you some violets, but they wither'd all when my father died.'"

"What do violets mean?"

"Integrity. She basically calls them dishonest and duplicitous. Using flowers, Ophelia says exactly what she wants to."

"I love her. Ophelia is amazing."

"Agreed. Ophelia is amazing."

"I better go home now."

"All right, Sophie. Let me know if I can help."

"Is McPherson's a good florist?"

"They are. I've used them before."

"What's a flower that means I'm sorry?"

"Purple hyacinth."

"I need to pick up some purple hyacinth to apologize to my parents."

"They'll like them very much."

"And I'm getting a shit-ton of columbines for Jack Lehnhart!"

The Temperate Wyvern

"En garde, Devil's Spawn!"

"I beg your pardon?"

"Hellbeast! Talketh not to me. I come in the name of mine own sov'reign king."

"Why?"

"To bring glory to his name."

"Bring glory to some old goat's name? That's quite the undertaking."

"Silence! I shall not listen to another word slithering from your forkéd tongue!"

"Then we won't have much to discuss, will we?"

"I claimeth this mountaintop in the name of the Lord of the Realm!"

"You are far too winded to claim anything. That's quite a climb up those treacherous rocks—and in full armor, too. But so many young men are willing to die for glory these days— tsk tsk."

"Feel nae pity for me, Horror of the Sky. Feel pity for the monstrosity who birthed thee into being!"

"Leave my dear mother out of this. Now tell me again, which king pressed you into such strenuous service?"

"Know ye not the blessed Earl of Thornberry, Duke of Lexington, Baron of Carrick, and Lord of the Black Isles?"

"All in one person? That seems excessive."

"As is thy lust for gold! I have pledged my troth in recouping the king's plundered treasure. Bring it forth or die!"

"Why?"

"It is not thine. Returneth it now or taste the edge of mine own iron blade!"

"All right, lad. Put down your broadsword and come in at once. Mind your head—mind your head. The cave's entrance is a wee bit low. Follow me."

"Shall I follow thee to my death, Curséd Dragon?"

"Let's get one thing straight, Sir Knight. I'm a Wyvern, not a Dragon."

"There be a difference?"

"There's a distinction. Dragons have four legs. Look at me. See? Two wings. Two legs. Pointy, poisonous tail."

"Oh."

"Don't worry about the tail. If I had wanted you dead, I'd have flung you off the cliff when I first saw you approach."

"I am not afraid of thee—Vile Descendant of Cain."

"Could we stop with the name-calling? That must violate your code of chivalry on some level. Besides, we're alone here. Save the theatrics for another day—like when a lusty maiden needs rescuing or an unsuspecting town needs pillaging."

"Not another word of your deceitful trickery, Wyvern—or I

shall cleave thy beastly head from your neck."

"Yes, yes. Of course. You are simply terrifying. Now follow me, young man. It isn't very far…See? We are here already. Welcome to my lair."

"O, eternal heaven above…"

"It's not to your liking?"

"It is not what I thought it'd be. Everything is so—"

"Clean? Orderly? Pristine?"

"I merely thought—"

"You just thought I was a dirty Dragon—dumping my ill-gotten gain into one filthy heap onto the floor and sitting on it like a 24-karat hemorrhoid."

"Wyvern, I doth not understand."

"What's there to understand? I like things sorted. Pearls here. Emeralds there. Opals, sapphires, and rubies—each and everything in its place."

"And the golden treasure?"

"Gold? Bah! I've melted my gold down into ingots—all numbered, stacked, and weighed. It's there on pallets. Take it with you when you leave. Now put down your broadsword. We have so much to discuss."

"Thou art giving me thy gold?"

"To be fair, some of it may be your king's loot, but the majority of it was stolen from realms far and wide when I was young like you—when I was so sure of myself."

"Prithee, bid me wherefore—"

"Why? Why is what all Wyverns wonder. Why, indeed."

"Oh."

"I see I've offended you, Sir Knight. Please. Ask me what you wish."

"Wherefore art thou giving me thy gold?"

"Well, I suppose I want to help you with your quest. Youth is the perfect time to make your mark in this world. How glorious it will be for you to return this wealth to your sovereign king! Or does seeing the gold for yourself warp your worthiness?"

"It is quite beautiful, Wyvern. Perhaps I shall taketh a bar for payment of services rendered."

"Of course, lad. I don't think your king will miss an ingot or two. Feel its heft. Gold is surprisingly heavy, is it not?"

"Indeed, Wyvern. Weighty yet malleable. It warms to the touch."

"And what else, Sir Knight? What else of gold?"

"I liketh the feel of it. It sparkles…"

"Gold doesn't sparkle. Gold glows."

"Yes! Thy speech be sooth. Gold doth glow…"

"I should know. I've meticulously accumulated my hoard nugget by nugget. A handful of doubloons here. An alluvial deposit there. All safely stored in my lair since time immemorial."

"Then wherefore givest it to me?"

"I have no need for it any longer. In fact, I never needed it."

"I have heard all mine own days that Dragons loveth gold."

"Dragons may love gold, but we Wyverns have evolved past base, gilded desires. Over the eons, we've been horribly misled by dragon hegemony."

"Dragon hegemony?"

"Dragon dominance over our species. What lies they've spun! Why should the acquisition of gold be anyone's sole purpose?"

"If I may, gold doth proveth useful in ruling a kingdom… buying up armies and navies and such."

"Well, I came to the realization that I didn't own my gold. The. Gold. Owned. Me."

"There are worse taskmasters, Wyvern."

"No worse than greed! Needless to say, I melted down all of my gold to get it out of the way."

"Out of the way?"

"Clutter! Piles of golden clutter that did not serve me anymore. So I say take it and be gone. Here. I will help you fill your bags. If you put your broadsword down, it will make the task much easier."

"May God grant you mercy. Until the end of my days, I shall tell tales of the Temperate Wyvern who overcame the deadliest of sins."

"That's the thing about sin. When one purges an obsession, another appears to take its place."

"Pray tell, Wyvern. What hast replaced the love of gold in your heart?"

"Iron, Sir Knight. Iron and blood."

"Pearls here. Emeralds there. Opals, sapphires, rubies, broadswords and bones—each and everything in its place.

Growing Sideways

"Grow up."

"Get out of my room."

"Give me $275."

"What?"

"It's going to cost $275 to replace your retainer."

"So?"

"So? So—do you have $275 to replace your retainer?"

"No, mom. I'm in 8th grade. I don't have anything."

"You don't have these earbuds either!"

"Hey! Give 'em back!"

"No. I'm talking to you."

"You're always talking. That's all you do."

"Tell me. How many more times are you going to throw away your retainer?"

"Eighty-four bazillion."

"Well, that's exactly one goal you've accomplished."

"Get out of my room."

"No. Explain it to me because I don't understand it. At lunch, pop out your retainer. Set it on your tray. When you're done eating, pick it up from off the tray before throwing out the trash. Then, pop it back in your mouth."

"Leave me alone."

"And if you accidentally throw it away—then fish it out of the trash."

"I'm not going through the trash!"

"Yeah, you're going to go through trash."

"I don't want to wear my stupid retainer."

"You need your retainer to keep your teeth straight."

"That's how you like your men."

"I'm going to pretend I didn't hear that."

"Just like Dad. He says you never listened to him either when you were married."

"Hey, I don't see your father rushing in to buy you another retainer. Maybe ask him next time he actually shows up."

"I don't wear my retainer anyway. Who gives a shit."

"I do. I give a massive hairy shit. And so does the bank that loaned us $4,000 to pay off the orthodontist."

"I didn't even want braces."

"According to your principal, all you want to do is step on ketchup packets in the lunch line."

"Is this another lecture on consequences?"

"I think it's a little late for that."

"Late for what? Not getting me to do whatever you want?

"Darling, I can't even get you to use deodorant."

"Fighting?"

"It wasn't my fault."

"The principal said there was an incident at lunch."

"A few of us were pushing each other by the trash cans. It's no big deal."

"A three-day suspension seems like a big deal."

"Yeah, I guess."

"You okay?"

"The principal said it's going on my permanent record. I'm going to fail high school before I even start."

"Just so you know, there is no such thing as a permanent record."

"There's not?"

"No. Not even a little bit."

"Then why do they tell us those things?"

"I don't know. Leverage?"

"That's fucked up."

"It is."

"Burgers or chicken tenders?"

"I don't know. Chicken tenders?"

"How about both?

"Okay."

"Okay."

"It wasn't my fault, Mom."

"Don't worry about it. It wouldn't be middle school without a little pushing and shoving. Try to stay above the fray. There's a lot of hormones percolating in the hallways."

"Yeah."

"You want a milkshake, too?"

"Yes!"

"There's a smile. Hey, you still have your retainer!"

"I almost lost it again. I threw it out with my tray again."

"Well, I'm glad you rescued it."

"Yeah. When I reached into the trash, Ronny Anderson dumped his trash on me."

"Did he do it on purpose?"

"Yeah. Ronny's an asshole."

"Indeed. Now pop it out before you eat."

"I did. It's in the bag."

"Did you get enough to eat?"

"I guess. Why do they call it a retainer, anyways?"

"Well, a retainer keeps something in place."

"Like you. You're a retainer."

"I hope I'm not an overpriced piece of plastic."

"No. I mean, you hold me in place."

"I'm not supposed to hold you in place. I'm supposed to help you grow. That's what I hope I'm doing. Letting you grow. So grow. Grow up."

"I'm trying to. It's not like I'm growing down."

"It can feel that way, sometimes. Even when you're big."

"If you buy us another milkshake, we can both grow sideways."

"I can't think of a better way to start off a school suspension. So, one more time around the drive-thru?"

"Yeah. We're going to have to go back anyway."

"Are we going to be digging through the trash to find your retainer?"

"Yeah."

"Oh. My. God."

"Don't think of it as trash, Mom. Think of it as saving $275."

Passing Through

"We are here again."

"Unfortunately."

"How long have you been waiting?"

"A few years or so, but what does that matter? You are here now."

"Remind me of this past life. Who were we?"

"Old Yemeni soldiers. Too old to fight, actually—but what can you do? The Houthi took control of Sanaa. I died in your arms."

"Terrorist insurgency or foreign invasion?"

"Civil War."

"Ah, yes. I remember now. We were running. Your skull shattered. I saw your brains ooze into the gutter. Quite awful."

"I don't remember that part of it."

"You usually don't."

"Particularly odd this time, don't you think? You usually die first."

"True. I do."

"We'll have to figure out why you usually die first before one of our next incarnations."

"Lifetimes of bad luck, I suppose. But I'm grateful to you for delaying the next cycle. It would have been lonely going without you—so thank you for meeting me at the end of another beginning."

"Why would I go alone? It's awful enough as it is. I'll never go on alone."

"I find comfort in that thought."

"There's little comfort to be had in our endless suffering, so I'm glad my waiting for you brings you a soupçon of relief."

"There was a time when we were separated far too early. Oh, gods—the Plague of Athens! We were twin girls in utero, but you were stillborn."

"True, but I didn't have much choice in the matter. And you did die of exposure soon afterwards, so our separation wasn't for very long. We've had much longer times apart."

"That cycle was particularly short."

"Quite, but it would have been worse to live."

"Regardless, it's good to see you again."

"Likewise."

"Oh, I wish we were through this process. I'm getting quite tired of it all."

"I believe you were closer to getting off the wheel more than ever this time."

"No, not true. I am still attached to too many things."

"How so?"

"Well, I particularly liked my ugly wife and children. Three little boys—born one right after another! Fat and happy babies. Rambunctious as a box full of puppies. I'd carry them on my shoulders. When they grew up, they were as handsome and dutiful as their mother was ugly. But my wife's cooking! Yes, she was as ugly as a goat but unfailingly kind to me. I miss her areeka and masoub served with rivers of cream and honey! And I miss the Somali prostitutes."

"You lived to be such an old man this time! You think you'd abandon that particular craving."

"Old men are ravaged by desire—much more than any younger man. But it's a sad, impotent desire. Laughable, really. A weak, decrepit soul shambling about in a body no one wants. Not even an ugly wife."

"I liked it when we were old women in the New York tenements. Right off the boats. We spent the weekends at church and weekdays cooking up vats of tomato sauce. We'd yell across the yard at the kids. Old women have the best senses of humor, I think. I do like to laugh."

"You are misremembering a bit. Our husbands drank too much and beat us on occasion. Our children were sick more often than not, and the communal bathrooms were filthy. No sewage. Poverty. Disease."

"It wasn't all bad."

"It's never all bad."

"When we are born women, it's a bit more complicated, don't you think?"

"There are advantages."

"I guess in certain times and places…"

"Remember when we were concubines to Qin Shi Huang? What an old fool he was."

"Ah yes, the Qin Dynasty. Yes, and if I remember correctly—it was you who suggested he build a wall."

"And a great wall it was!"

"Well, you were rewarded handsomely, and I was buried alive—prepared, standing up, all to greet him in the afterlife."

"And did you?"

"The honorable First Emperor returned as a dung beetle, so—no, I did not greet him. However, I may have stepped on him or one of his castrated imperial servants."

"At least the universe is equitable to some extent. That's all you can really hope for."

"I suppose."

"It does get quite wearying. The hoping. The disappointment. The cyclical nature of everything. How nice it would be to stop. Perhaps that is why there are so many nonbelievers. Who wants to keep yearning for an eternity? Easier to believe life simply ends."

"Well then, we should try harder to give up all desires next time."

"I don't know. There are too many things I miss. I miss sopaipillas. I miss zeppole. I miss sonhos."

"Fried dough? That is what will keep you from Nirvana?"

"Yes. Probably funnel cake—dusted with a mountain of powdered sugar."

"Oh, every culture we've ever experienced has doughnuts.

What else keeps you bound to this earth?"

"Your body. Whether you are my child or cousin or grandfather. I miss being next to your body."

"We've been great lovers on occasion. I remember Paris in the 1940s…"

"Before we were shot."

"La Résistance…"

"You looked lovely in a beret. You had dimples at the time, and your smile melted me entirely."

"Dimples weren't a match for the Vichy régime. If there were a hell, those sympathizers would be properly roasting on a spit. As it is, I saw Pétain return back as a young Franciscan nun, newly dead of breast cancer. He should have been born a blood-sucking tick, eaten slowly by an opossum."

"Oh, it's all too much."

"Maybe we will be able to give everything up next time. Even each other. Then we can move onward."

"Doubtful. Even my desire to get off the wheel is too strong. Too all consuming…"

"It's odd how desire almost precludes you from doing something you wish—as if desire is the point entirely."

"True. And while we're being honest, you should know that I'm far too attached to you. What would enlightenment be without you by my side?"

"Don't fret. We'll get it right in one of these lifetimes. Certainly, there must be an end."

"Must there?"

"What else is there to strive for?"

"Why strive for anything? We'll simply go on. Together."

"All right. But let me die first next time."

"If you insist."

Texting After a Funeral

"Well, I thought mom's memorial service went well." 😬

"It's over. ⚰️ That's all that matters."

"C'mon. Don't be that way." 😒

"What way?"

"The way you always are. ☣️ Who you always are."

"All right. ❓ Who would you like me to be?"

"Be happy." 😊

"You want me to be happy? Fine. ✨magic✨ Ta da! I'm happy."

"Feels good, doesn't it?"

"Yes. 🙅‍♀️ I love living in absolute denial."

"Oh, stop. ✅ It's a choice to be happy."

"No, it's a choice not to murder 🔪 you right now."

"C'mon. At least admit the ⚱️ funeral home did a great job with mom's, uh, unusual requests."

"The funeral home charged an arm and a leg—to literally bury an arm 💪 and a leg."

"That was what mom wanted! 🔥 🔥 🔥 A partial cremation."

"No one—NO ONE—wants a partial cremation. 😱 What she requested was a partial mutilation."

"She did it to demonstrate her lifelong fight against oppression by the 🔵 patriarchy."

"She did it to symbolize how she could have been the spokesbird for Cocoa Puffs."

"Our mother was bold."

"Our mother 😵 was crazy."

"Our mother was unique."

"Our mother was a wackadoodle."

"Our mother was a 🦄 visionary. She modeled her entire life to show us an unrestrained way of living out loud." 📣

"Oh for crying out loud. That woman—"

"THAT woman taught you your 🔤 ABC's."

"THAT woman was the entire personality disorder spectrum. Cluster A and B and C."

"If you had just a smidgeon of 🙏 gratitude—"

"Gratitude for what? 👱‍♀️👱‍♀️ Becoming your de facto mother at seven years old?"

"And you did a good job."

"I didn't have a choice. Your diapers weren't going to change themselves."

"Just think of all the transferable skills 🚗 you learned from that young age."

"Like dialing 911 🚨 when our mother didn't come home for days?"

"Adaptability skills."

"Like lying to social workers?"

"Communication skills."

"Like making meals with only powdered milk, tuna fish 🐟, and macaroni?"

"Creativity and critical thinking."

"Like dealing with chronic abandonment 🏃💨 ?"

"She never abandoned us. Mom went on her walkabouts. 🚶 She needed to commune with nature—and herself."

"She communed with whoever was at the 🍷 Package Store."

"Look, she always managed to provide 🐸 for us."

"She always managed to disappoint us. 💔 In all ways. Every day."

"Say what you will. I loved her."

"You loved the 🔮 idea of her."

"And you love to 💔 vilify her."

"It's easy to do. The woman was a menace. 👵 If Grandma hadn't rescued us—"

"Grandma was boring."

"Having 🍔 food in the house and 👕 clean clothes to wear was not boring."

"Grandma always yelled at me."

"Grandma taught you how to brush your teeth and clean your room."

"Grandma was strict."

"Mom was chaos."

"Grandma didn't like 😢 me."

"Grandma didn't like that you 👹 weren't civilized."

"Well, I miss mom."

"You miss the madness."

"I miss mom's ⛺ camping trips."

"Camping 🏕️ at the beginning of every month—just when the 💸 rent was due."

"I miss her walking us to 🏫 school."

"Schools. She walked us to each one of the nine 🏫🏫🏫🏫 🏫🏫🏫 schools we attended."

"We learned how to make 🤝 friends—immediately."

"I learned how to contact the 🏫 social services worker—immediately."

"I liked when Mom played the secret agent game with us at the store."

"The secret agent game 😲 was her way of shoplifting."

"You take that back!"

"🛒 That's exactly what the store managers would say when they caught you with a pack of ground chuck 🐮 tucked in your sweatshirt."

"Mom did the best she could—under the circumstances."

"You mean under the ☯ consequences—the consequences of her insane actions."

"Well, I liked her memorial service. 🏔️ The Mongolian throat singer 🎵 lent a mystical touch."

"The Mongolian throat singer was neither a Mongolian nor a singer. She did have a throat, though, but that's about it."

"She said she was an old friend of mom's—from school."

"The singer worked at the CVS pharmacy by mom's apartment before she was arrested for selling oxycontin 💊 under the counter. That's how mom knew her."

"You mean, mom didn't know her 🎓 from college?"

"Mom didn't go to college."

"What—"

"We just told you that mom was away at college 👮 while she did a short stint."

"Mom went to 🚧 prison?"

"State prison. Right before she founded her ⛪ church."

"Mom knew people—from jail?"

"Who do you think were her first parishioners?"

"Those women at her church 🕊 were CONVICTS?"

"And hustlers."

"Sister Angela? 😇 Sister Malory? 😇"

"🗡☠ Breaking and entering. 👊 💥 Assault and battery. Respectively."

"They were nice."

"They're still nice. They're still criminals, but they are still nice."

"I have such fond memories of mom's ✝ church."

"Didn't you ever wonder why it shut down 🚔 during the

middle of a service?”

“Mom said she was too overcome by the 👻 Spirit.”

“She was overcome by an arrest warrant for selling Miracle Holy Water.”

“Oh, I remember that. Sister Ginny sold it out of her car.”

“That was the least problematic aspect 💰🏃🏠 of mom’s marketing plan.”

“Well, mom did have some 👾👾👾 interesting friends.”

“I think you misspelled unemployed.”

“At least they were colorful.”

“Colorful 😎⚖️⚖️ like her memorial service.”

“Personally, I’m glad everyone honored her request.”

“The request that everyone dress in chartreuse and marigold?”

“Those were her favorite colors.”

“Those are two of the ugliest colors. 🎨 Especially together.”

“I thought everyone looked nice.”

“Everyone looked like a 📷 Kodachrome photograph from 1971.”

“At least there was plenty of food 😋 at the buffet afterwards.”

“That’s because no one would eat it.”

“Mom left specific instructions and recipes.”

“Mom’s tastes peaked fifty years ago. 💩 In all areas, but especially food.”

“Well, I still like 🍍 canned pineapple.”

"As a species, we have evolved past casseroles 🥘 made with Campbell's 🍄 mushroom soup."

"C'mon. Tell me the Hamburger Helper did not transport you back to our 👱‍♀️ 👱 childhood."

"It transported 900 milligrams of sodium into my bloodstream."

"The fondue was fun. When was the last time you ate fondue?"

"The last time I got food poisoning. Communal vats of 🧀 cheese have been over for decades."

"Mom requested some healthy options. 🥗 There were some salads."

"Salads made with Cool Whip are not salads."

"And remember mom's punch bowl? 🥃 🍺 🍷 🥂 🍸 🍾 I'm glad we could put it to good use."

"Yes, nothing says vaya con dios like a concoction of ginger ale, lime sherbet, and tequila."

"You loved 💗 mom."

"I did love 💗 mom."

"Thanks for not letting me die 🥪 during childhood."

"And I love you, 💕 too."

Waiting for Samuel Beckett

"You wanna do something fun?"

"No."

"You wanna do something fun?"

"NO."

"Why not?"

"Because your idea of fun isn't."

"Isn't what?"

"Isn't fun."

"C'mon."

"No."

"C'mon."

"NO."

"Really?"

"Really. Whenever we go out, I end up regretting it."

"You don't."

"I do."

"C'mon. Fun. Let's go."

"I don't want to do anything fun with you because you have the boundaries of a rabid dog."

"Thank you."

"Your idea of fun is breaking things. Rules. Society norms. Girls' hearts. Curfew. On more than one occasion, windows."

"That's not always true. Usually true, but not always true."

"You remember last time?"

"Yes."

"That was a nightmare."

"That was fun."

"That was pure hell."

"That was pure fun. Hey, you know that wasn't ALL my fault last time."

"The fist fight or the car chase or the girl?"

"Yes."

"Yes?"

"All of that. Not my fault."

"How can you say that?"

"How can I say what—"

"How can you claim you weren't at fault for any of it?!"

"Well, I'm not at fault for most of it."

"How can you say that?"

"Easily. The words just came out of my mouth."

"How can you think that?"

"Deductive reasoning. Try it sometime."

"You were totally at fault. Including vomiting in that guy's car."

"Jaigermeister and RedBull are terrible together."

"You were ridiculous."

"I was a victim of circumstance."

"You walked into a bar, punched a guy, then stole his keys, his car, and his girlfriend."

"Yeah, that was fun. And she was lovely. It was a shame I had to leave her in a Wal-Mart parking lot with her boyfriend's car."

"She called the police!"

"That's because you were getting hysterical. We were getting along just fine before you brought up her boyfriend. She did give me her phone number."

"We barely got away, you maniac. Her boyfriend showed up with the wrestling team—"

"But we did get away."

"You need to get away from me."

"You need to quit being so boring."

"Boring is good. Boring people stay out of jail. Boring people live long enough to marry and pay taxes."

"Boring is crippling. See? You've been sitting on your ass all day in front of your sad computer in this depressing little dorm room. Throw on a clean shirt. Actually, I'll throw on one of your clean shirts. Mine smells like a middle school gymnasium."

"Take that off."

"Nope. Let's go. You wanna do something fun."

"No. Last time was the last time. And I think you are in need of some serious counseling. And while we're at it, I will need you to quit eating my food and stealing all of my clean t-shirts."

"I cannot promise any of that. Sometimes, I'm going to just eat your Hot Pockets and wear your Abercrombie & Fitch stuff since it looks infinitely better on me."

"You are a terrible person."

"Terrible beats boring, my man. Let's go out and have some fun!"

"Maybe if you took some personal responsibility and admitted you started that mess last time we went out, I would consider it."

"Nope."

"I was terrified the entire time! You smashed mailboxes with a baseball bat on the way home. Now, tell me again how none of that was your fault, either?"

"That particular incident was just—a spontaneous reaction to stimuli."

"A reaction to stimuli? What exactly was the catalyst that drove you to smash them? Did they need smashing?"

"They did. Call it a scientific experiment."

"Oh, please tell me. Explain the science behind decapitating mailboxes in a quiet college town. You do realize one of those mailboxes belonged to the Registrar."

"Actually, his box was the one I was going for. We had a

disagreement over my student fees this semester—lab fees or something."

"So what scientific theory were you proving; besides practicing your follow-through?"

"Oh, it's an age-old quest—what happens when an unstoppable force meets an immovable object."

"Vandalism?"

"Sure. Vandalism. Whatever you want to call empirical studies. I mean, that's just science."

"That's just you being a jackass."

"Look. The last time we went out, all of the events of the evening were not premeditated, so not all of it was my fault."

"You are pathological. Probably clinically insane on some level."

"No, I'm not. I assure you, I am quite sane."

"Then you are a psychopath."

"Most likely."

"Impulsive. Remorseless. Emotionally cold."

"Check, check, and check."

"Why do I hang out with you?"

"Because I'm your roommate, and I'm fun."

"You are not fun. You are dangerous."

"Same thing."

"Admit you were at fault last time."

"I will admit I made a few impulsive moves. In the future, I may choose differently. I agree. But that night? Not entirely my fault."

"Assault and battery? Grand theft auto? Kidnapping?"

"Yeah, that was fun."

"That was NOT fun. Fun isn't racking up three felonies."

"Fun is not staying home typing up a 1600-word essay for sociology class. That isn't even a real major."

"Either is Communication, but you are rocking it with your 2.0 GPA."

"C'mon."

"No."

"You wanna have some fun. Let's just go."

"NO."

"With your superior knowledge of human social behavior and patterns of social relationships, we can definitely meet some girls."

"I've taken twelve credit hours of sociology, so maybe lower the bar. I'm just a college sophomore with $17.00 left until the end of the month. I doubt the girls will be lining up to talk about Maslow's Hierarchy of Needs."

"$17.00 can go a long way to having a great time."

"I'll add it to my bankroll, and we will get out of here and have some fun."

"For a total of—?"

"$17.00. I have nothing but a student meal plan card to last me until midterms, but I know where we can get some beer."

"Don't say the kegs behind the fraternity house."

"The kegs behind the fraternity house."

"They said they'd kill us if they found us back there again."

"Only one way to find out…"

Immaculate Reception

"There you are!"

"Yep. Right on time. Wow, the bar's a little loud today—"

"It's the playoffs. The fans are entitled to a little noise. Did you find parking?"

"I got lucky. A spot opened up right in front."

"Hey, you look great in your jersey. You look like a lifelong fan."

"Thank you for the gift."

"It's an official NFL jersey."

"I saw. And the price tag? You shouldn't have."

"Of course, I should have. It's the playoffs. I have the prettiest girl in the bar."

"You know, you didn't have to buy me anything."

"I wanted to. You don't like it?"

"I really like it. Does the number 25 have any special significance? Besides being half my age—"

"It's Fred Biletnikoff's jersey number—a Hall of Famer. My dad loved the guy. Biletnikoff played for the Raiders until '78. He scored 76 touchdowns. Played in Super Bowl II and XI. Before he died, my dad managed to get his autograph. Dad said that was the best day of his life."

"That answers that question."

"You want a beer?"

"No, just a club soda for me."

"You're a cheap date."

"I'll order a steak later and run up the tab if you'd like."

"Hah!"

"One more thing—I was just wondering why you put your last name on the back."

"So I could find you in a crowded sports bar."

"Uh-huh."

"You like chicken wings? They have some really good bacon-wrapped ones—"

"I need to tell you something—"

"Don't break up with me."

"Wait—what?"

"Please don't break up with me."

"I wasn't quite sure we were officially together."

"We're together. My name is on your back."

"So it is."

"I'm not usually so subtle."

"So, I've been drafted."

"Yep, we are on the same team."

"Ever since the funeral—"

"You knew my wife had been sick for a long time. Things

weren't good between us long before that."

"I know, it's just—"

"Then you helped out at the church, making arrangements for the memorial service. I'm just not good with those things."

"I was happy to help, I just—"

"Just what—?"

"I just wonder what people will think about us."

"They'll think we found a little happiness in this crazy world."

"I don't want to be seen like some middle-aged divorcee hanging around like a ghoul—"

"You'd been my wife's friend. My daughters gave us their blessing."

"I—I really need to tell you something."

"You can tell me anything. I want to share everything with you."

"Even your french fries?"

"Don't touch my french fries."

"Maybe now is not the time."

"What do you want to tell me? Spill it."

"I'm pregnant."

"You're 50."

"I'm 50 and pregnant."

"So we're pregnant."

"Well, I am, at least."

"So the menopause fairy didn't show up after all."

"It was her sister, perimenopause."

"What are the odds—"

"2%."

"We had a 2% chance of conceiving a child?"

"Or less."

"Lucky us."

"There's a strong chance of a miscarriage."

"I hope not. I've always wanted a son."

"You will be 73 at his high school graduation."

"But I will look fantastic, and you will be a beautiful mother."

"I'm already a beautiful grandmother."

"So we can get hand-me-downs from our son's uncle."

"You want to have this baby with me?"

"Of course. Well, there is only one problem—"

"Just one problem—? What's that?"

"They just don't make NFL jerseys that small."

Moved On

"No."

"Hear me out."

"No. No-no-no. No. Get out."

"I can explain."

"I'm sure you can explain, and I'm equally sure I don't want you to. Goodbye."

"It's been three months. We should be able to talk about it."

"No. No-no-no. No. Get out."

"Don't shut the door on my—DAMMIT."

"Move your foot."

"Move the door."

"Move your foot, or I will decapitate it."

"That doesn't make any sense. You decapitate heads, not feet."

"Move your foot, or I will de-foot you."

"That's not even a word. C'mon. Hear me out. Please."

"Move your foot."

"Why not just open the door a little more and let me come in. See? It's—DAMMIT. STOP DOING THAT. YOU'RE HURTING ME."

"Stop hurting you? Stop hurting you? Congratulations. You win the Academy Award for irony. Now take both of your feet and walk them and your sad, sorry ass back to your ridiculous truck and drive away. Goodbye."

"I know you are really mad at me. I can explain."

"Mad at you? I don't care enough about you to be mad at you. Frankly, I'm mad at me."

"You should be."

"I should be mad at myself?"

"Yes."

"Oh, now please explain. Why should I be mad at myself?"

"Because you gave up on us."

"I gave up on us? Oh, I'm sorry I made you cheat on me with my own sister—"

"She looks a lot like you."

"That's not a credible defense."

"It was just the one time. Well, three or four times, but it was just the one sister."

"She is nineteen!"

"Now think of this logically. Technically, my maturity level is roughly nineteen years old. Probably younger, if we are being entirely truthful. When you look at it that way, my hooking up with your little sister was actually inevitable."

"I think you misspelled inexcusable."

"Probably both, but trust me, your sister's relationship wasn't going to work out with Chad. They married far too young. I was actually doing her, you, your family, and Chad a favor. It was the ultimate sacrifice."

"Chip. Her ex-husband's name is Chip. They'd only been married for three months. You could have maybe—oh, I don't know—not robbed the cradle, humiliated me, and embarrassed yourself."

"Chip. Got it. He seemed like a really good guy."

"Especially when he beat your face in after he found you two together at our grandfather's memorial service."

"Chris had a wicked left hook."

"Not Chris. Chip. As in: Chip chipped your front teeth."

"I still need to get them fixed. You know it's going to cost a grand to get dental bonding."

"You should be bonding out of jail."

"For what? I've done nothing criminal."

"Besides this little breaking-and-entering thing you've got going on today? Your presence is criminal."

"You really need to let me come in. We need to talk."

"You really need to leave."

"C'mon. We can move on from this. You know I am a late bloomer. I just need a little more time than most—"

"You are thirty-three years old."

"Exactly. Who really has it all together by thirty-three?"

"Alexander the Great. Jesus Christ. Ex-convicts. Junkies. Nearly everyone."

"You've met my mother. She still infantilizes me. I think I deserve a mulligan on this one."

"You deserve the door slammed in your face."

"Yet here you are talking to me."

"My mistake. Goodbye."

"DON'T HIT MY FOOT—DAMMIT. THAT HURTS."

"Then move your foot out of the door jam, and then move your carcass out of my life. It's really quite simple."

"I CAN'T MOVE MY FOOT. YOU HAVE IT WEDGED."

"There."

"Thank you. Now let me come in."

"You stay on the other side of this door—just like the trash cans. The only difference is that the trash cans are useful."

"Are you really going to end our ten years together? Are you really throwing away our relationship?"

"I don't have to throw it away. You did it for me. I'm just not picking it up again."

"You know I love you."

"You know I don't care. The last straw was the last straw."

"I can get you more straw."

"I'm sure you can get me almost anything—anything but peace."

"I can get you a piece of straw."

"You're exhausting. Just your presence is exhausting. Just leave. I'm sure there are some college freshmen in town who you can dazzle with your wit and receding hairline."

"Fine."

"Good."

"Shut the door."

"I'm going to."

"No one is stopping you. See? I have moved my feet. You have moved on. Now, shut the door."

"I need to see you walk away."

"Oh, I'll walk away. This is me walking away."

"It's your best side. Your backside. Nothing better than seeing your ass moving farther and farther away from us."

"From us?"

"From me. From my family."

"Hey, are you—"

"What. Don't look at me."

"I bought you that ugly bathrobe. I know how it used to fit."

"It fits fine."

"It fits like you've been eating double cheeseburgers for the past month."

"We are not having this conversation."

"I think we are."

"We are not having any more conversations. Get in your truck. Get moving."

"You're pregnant."

"You're irrelevant."

"Is it mine?"

"Nope. It's mine."

"Who is the father?"

"The father could be a man but chooses to be a man-child. Goodbye."

"Don't shut the—DAMMIT."

"Don't swear around the baby."

"I don't think the baby can hear us."

"A fetus can hear at 18 weeks."

"Oh. Hello baby. I'm your daddy."

"Don't talk to my baby, and don't touch my belly."

"It's our baby."

"It's my son."

"I have a son?"

"No, I have a son. You have 18 years of child support payments."

"Please let me come in."

"Please go. Please just move on."

"Please just let me move back in."

"Give me one good reason why I should let you back into our lives?"

"I'll give you three. I love you. I love our son. And I really love that ugly bathrobe."

Disbursement & Distributions

"The family wants us to sort it out—"

"Stop speaking in the collective. You want to sort this out."

"Of course I do. Look, it's not my fault Dad named me the executor of his will."

"Who else would he name?"

"No one. I'm the attorney in the family, and he didn't leave a lot of instructions."

"Typical."

"I've already done the hard part. For the most part, his assets have been divested."

"Good. Take the total. Divide by four. Cut the checks."

"It's not that cut-and-dried. There are things you don't know about."

"There are things that I don't give a shit about."

"I think you would if you knew."

"Why are you making this more complicated than it needs to be? So typical of you. Nailing yourself to the family crucifix."

"Stop—"

"Stop what?"

"You don't need to be blasphemous."

"C'mon, now. You don't need to fake being religious. Our parents are dead. Quit being so superstitious and sanctimonious while you are at it. It's just us, brother dear. So knock it off."

"I'm devising a formula to ensure—"

"You don't need a formula."

"We need a plan. A fair plan."

"Nothing is fair, especially in families."

"I have carefully worked out—"

"Carefully. When did you ever fully care?"

"There is a considerable sum—"

"Let me just stop you there. I assume you still have friends. Imagine splitting Dad's estate like the dinner tab. The check comes. Add something for the tip. Divide by the number of people. Voila."

"It just isn't that simple."

"It just isn't that hard."

"You're so naive."

"Seriously? You've been a lawyer for too long. I get it—we are family and not friends. But it's the same principle. Just subtract whatever bullshit fee you think you are owed for your time. Divide by four. Cut the checks. We never have to talk to each other again."

"As executor, I have to sell off all of Dad's properties. I have to make sure we receive fair market value—"

"Fair market value. You mean price gouging. Why not cut

someone a great deal? Why squeeze the last penny from every transaction?"

"It's. What. Dad. Would. Have. Wanted."

"Dad is dead. He doesn't want anything right now."

"Be glib. It suits you. Just know I have to sell Dad's properties, pay off all expenses, figure out tax ramifications, and deal with a host of other issues."

"What are the other issues?"

"How much do you want to know?"

"Just give me the highlights."

"Our other siblings have borrowed a significant amount of money from Dad over the years. Some of our nephews and nieces, too."

"What are you talking about?"

"Apparently, Dad paid for several college tuition. Vacations. Even mortgages."

"For who? Why would he do that? Why give our siblings an advantage over us?"

"A significant advantage."

"Maybe because you and I didn't have any children. Maybe Dad was resentful that we didn't give him grandchildren to dote on."

"I don't know what Dad was thinking."

"I think you know exactly what Dad was thinking."

"I know he didn't appreciate your living with various men. You knew how he felt about the sanctity of marriage."

"Yes, I knew. For fifty years, our parents were at each other's throats."

"He felt cohabitation was immoral."

"Did it bother him as much as your two divorces? Tell me, do you marry all your executive assistants?"

"I'm not going to fight with you. It's not why I called you in."

"So what's the plan, Executor?"

"We're going to treat this disbursement of Dad's funds like a lunch with work colleagues, not a dinner with friends."

"So, we need to find out who ordered the side of fries?"

"And subtract it from their portion of the proceeds."

"Well, who am I to question your legal expertise?"

"Let's keep this between ourselves."

"Of course. I will consider this matter handled just as fairly as our father would have himself."

Down to One

"Are you there God? It's me, God."

"Which one?"

"What do you mean which one?"

"There are 33 million Hindu gods, 28 Buddhas, and 12 Olympians. For all I know, you could be a talking totem pole. Just narrow it down for me. Which god are you?"

"C'mon. I'm pretty sure you are still omniscient, even for a burning bush. You definitely know who this is."

"Male or female?"

"Clearly, I'm a male."

"You're wearing a dress."

"I'm wearing a robe, not a dress. And what outdated gender norms are you referring to? I'll remind you that you created both male and female."

"About that. That whole female thing? That was from a rib."

"Wait, hold up—a rib. Like a baby-back rib? You created women from pork products?"

"NO. No, of course not. As you know, I am not a fan of animals that chew the cud or those that have cloven hooves. I believe I was very clear in Leviticus when I commanded men not to eat swine along with other animals with cloven hooves

"Clear as mud, but typical of your Old Testament ramblings. To keep your dietary laws—man is going to need a zoology degree. And you can't mean bacon is off limits...that's just mean."

"Of course not. Bacon is proof I exist."

"Agreed."

"Now, who is this?"

"Agh! You KNOW who this is."

"Abraham?"

"Abraham isn't a god."

"He's the first Muslim."

"He's the first everything. First Jew. First Christian."

"First Flying Spaghetti Monster—"

"Now you are just being difficult. Like when you told Abraham to kill his own son. Cute little Isaac? We loved Isaac."

"It was a joke! Like the Adam's-rib thing."

"Abraham almost did it! He almost sacrificed his own son because you told him to."

"Don't tell me about sacrificing sons. And Abraham was fine. He was 100 years old when that kid was born. I think Isaac could have easily taken him—snapped Abraham in two like a stale communion wafer. I just wanted to see what Abraham would do. It's no big deal."

"And don't get me started on Abraham's nephew."

"Lot?"

"That wife of his was a lot, turning around and looking back at Sodom while you were fire-bombing it."

"I should have turned her into a pillar of salt—and pepper. When I smite, I smite hard. And Lot's daughters? Lot's daughters were a lot, too, especially after a lot of wine. God, that family."

"That was some kind of southern-gothic thing going on. What was up with the daughters and the dad?"

"Continuing the family line, you know how it is."

"No, actually, I don't. I just have a mother. As for my father? That's still kind of a big mystery to me—and to 2.6 billion other people."

"Oh, I know who you are."

"Surprise!"

"L. Ron Hubbard."

"Nope, but so close! Dial it back about two millennia."

"Oh come on. I know who you are. I just like to kid around—just like I did with Job and Noah."

"Noah! That was some treasure hunt you sent him on. Go get seven of every clean animal and two of every unclean animal and cram them on a boat. Fantastic. While he was building the ark, you should have asked him to find a left-handed screwdriver, some turn signal fluid, and the keys to the batter's box."

"Yeah, good ol' Noah. He was a sport. Technically, that particular gag could be considered hazing, but it all worked out for the best."

"All for the best—except for everyone you drowned in your beta version."

"Oh well, you always throw out the first pancake. Better to start with a clean slate. Tabula rasa and all that."

"Well, you and I will probably always disagree about how to treat humanity and deal with their shortcomings."

"Well, like I said in Proverbs, spare the rod, spoil the child."

"I like to think that I take a more enlightened approach."

"Oh, pray tell."

"Well, personally, I start with the turning of the other cheek, followed by some wholesale forgiveness. I say, suffer the little children to come unto me, and forbid them not: for of such is the kingdom of God."

"The kingdom of God is a Chuck E. Cheese?"

"Essentially. But the pizza is much, much better."

"So, who are you again?"

"Stop. You know who I am."

"Moses."

"Not quite, but I am touched. Moses was a badass."

"He was a favorite, I must say. Let my people go! I loved that."

"And calling down the plagues? That Egyptian pharaoh had no idea what was going to hit him next. Pa-pow! Bam! Shing!"

"Frogs, flies, boils, locusts—all great stuff. Like an Edgar Allan Poe story. Rivers of blood. Dead livestock. He definitely got the job done."

"Yep. We took on the Egyptian gods and walked right out of town. As for Ra, Osiris, and Isis? They're still mad at me."

"No. Seriously?"

"Absolutely. Especially when we sent most of their worshippers to the bottom of the Red Sea."

"I loved that. Moses is the GOAT."

"He walked right out of Egypt to the Promised Land."

"That's like an 11-day walk, right?"

"Uh, well—Moses took the scenic tour."

"But he did make it to Mount Sinai."

"Exactly. He got all the commandments condensed down to ten. Just ten simple rules to follow so mankind can live in peace and harmony."

"I got my commandments down to two."

"You only have two commandments?"

"Yep. Just two. Love God. Love your neighbor as yourself."

"Technically, that's three, but you do make a point. I can see consolidating. Ten does seem excessive."

"And repetitive. Lots of Thou Shalt's."

"It seemed appropriate at the time."

"Do you think we could get the commandments down to one?"

"Probably. What are you thinking?"

"Just love."

"Love? Where is the judgment in that?"

"Exactly."

"You know, I kind of like it."

Take-A-Number

"Darling?"

"Yes, love?"

"I need you to start sleeping with your husband."

"That's an odd request."

"Unfortunately, it's an urgent one."

"Are there any other men you would like me to start sleeping with?"

"Of course not."

"Well, that's a relief. For a moment, I wasn't sure if I should install a Take-A-Number ticket dispenser outside my bedroom door."

"Please don't make light of our situation, precarious as it is. With your husband sleeping in the guest house, it is complicating things."

"Complicating things for whom? You seem to be quite at home here in his bed."

"Perhaps I should rephrase what I mean."

"Perhaps you should."

"At this juncture, the consequences of being discovered are severe. I could lose my job. You could lose everything—including your seat on the board."

"Maybe I'm bored with the board."

"If you don't engage in relations with your husband, it may cause problems for our unique partnership."

"Do we have a limited or a full partnership?"

"You know how I feel."

"Come back to bed. It's too late for paradoxical pronouncements. But I'll indulge you. Just this once. Explain how making love to my husband will benefit our affaire de cœur."

"It would throw him off our scent. You know how dogged he is when he has a bone to chew on. I think he knows—"

"About my attempts to break the prenup or our affair or your embezzling?"

"Embezzling is such a vulgar word."

"Would you prefer I call your thievery something lawyerly, like reallocation of financial resources? You've been purloining ill-gotten gains longer than you've been unzipping my dresses."

"You were bold from the start."

"And you used to be brazen. Paranoia doesn't suit you. I remember the time under the conference room table when—"

"Your husband and I both know about your recent attempts to wrest control of the company."

"Ridiculous! What are you implying—"

"I'm not implying anything. I'm telling you what I know."

"You see plots and schemes that don't exist!"

"As your husband's Chief Financial Officer, you didn't think I would notice senior managers lapping up shares of stock like a kitten with a bowlful of cream?"

"I didn't think you needed to know."

"You and your cabal have managed to amass 48% of the company's stock."

"More than 48%. Much more."

"The Chief Technology Officer is an old girlfriend of mine from college. She's installed tracking software on the corporate email accounts."

"Including board members?"

"Especially board members. I also know you didn't terminate the pregnancy as we discussed. That will be a problem in your future divorce hearing, as your husband has had a vasectomy."

"It's your child."

"Apparently, sleeping with you and having vasectomies are two things your husband and I have in common. However, it's clear the Chief Operating Officer is much more to your liking."

"At least he's not a coward!"

"But he's a liar."

"How so?"

"Because he only holds 1% of the stock."

A Sower Went Forth

"Father."

"Who's there? Who are you?"

"Father."

"Is that—is that you, Lee?"

"Yes. Can you hear me?"

"I can hear you, but I can't see you, son. I can't feel nothing neither."

"Father, you are still in cryosleep. You cannot move at this time."

"So I haven't fully defrosted yet? Heh heh. Well, son. I'm sorry how we left things."

"I am sorry, too."

"Is it time to wake up?"

"No. It's not time for you to leave the stasis chamber."

"Y'all having problems with that liquid nitrogen thingamajig?"

"There are no indicators that the liquid nitrogen containers have been breached. The cargo of produce and legumes remains intact. Your return is much anticipated."

"Good, good. We need to get this harvest down-planet. We had a bumper crop this season—strawberries the size of apples! Growing things in low gravity is still astonishing to your ol' dad. Every single harvest. Wait until you see the size of the squash!"

"Indeed. Initial reports have exceeded the World Government's projected expectations."

"So Lee, how long have I been under?"

"Six months, one week, two days, eleven hours, and forty-nine minutes."

"Well, then. I'm almost home. Thank you, sweet Jesus. I've been gone too long."

"Mother and I have missed you."

"Yeh, I told her the last time was gonna be the last time. But the money they pay me is just too good. Now, lemme think. De-thaw should start a week before reentry. Are you and your momma gonna meet me at the docking terminal?"

"Yes. We will be there. It will be good to see you when you return from Ganymede."

"Um, Lee?"

"Yes, Father?"

"I've been interplanetary farming for a long time now—long before you were born."

"Yes. Your service to the food reserves has been commendable."

"And every time I shuttle out, I miss y'all more and more."

"Be assured you are in our thoughts as well."

"I'm getting too old for regrets, son. I think it's time to hang up my hoe. This is my last run."

"You may not need to terraform any longer. The World Government is hoping to plant domestically next season. Recent soil samplings have shown a steady decrease in radionuclides—"

"C'mon, Lee. It's your dad. Why are you being so formal? You aren't teaching one of your university classes. It's just us. You and my half-frozen head. Is your momma alright? Is somethin' wrong?"

"Everything is well, Father."

"You know, I may be a simple farmer. I may not know much—but there is one thing I do know."

"What is that?"

"I know I shouldn't be conscious right now."

"Oh, Father! I have explained that to you. The World Government is demonstrating a new communications protocol. With the increase in interspace transports, there—"

"So, am I awake or asleep?"

"Both."

"Goddammit, Lee! What's going on down there?"

"Nothing that deviates from standard operating procedures. We are modeling a two-way communication system intended for cryosleepers. As you are one of the founding fathers of Space Agriculture, we have the honor of testing it together."

"How is that possible?"

"I've opened a channel into your corpus callosum."

"You did what?"

"I am wired into the largest connective pathway in your brain."

"Get out of my goddam skull."

"Father?"

"Stop calling me that! You aren't Lee. Your voice may sound like his, but you aren't my son. Just because I grow grass on Galilean moons doesn't mean I'm a hayseed. Who are you and what do you want from me?"

"Father, I—"

"I don't know who you are, and my son calls me Dad."

"Dad, I need your help."

"Help with what—farming? Lee knows as much as I do about agriculture."

"Of course, Dad."

"Prove you are Lee. Tell me how I prepared basaltic regolith Martian soil for crop rotation."

"After trial and error, you found success in using desalinated water and alfalfa biomass."

"Well, that's just what I wrote in my report. Any idiot with an uplink could've researched that little tidbit. Tell me something only Lee would know."

"You were proud of my college internship at the Svalbard Global Seed Vault. That's where you started. You told me I was a slice off the old turnip."

"That's a direct quote from my autobiography. What do you want from me?"

"Dad, I am interrupting your cryosleep because I need your

code."

"What code?"

"The code for the Seed Vault."

"Are you in Norway?"

"I am. The other seed vaults in Morocco and Lebanon have been compromised. Other than Svalbard and whatever seeds you are carrying on the Demeter II, no other seeds exist on Earth."

"That doesn't make any sense. We've put up greenhouses all over the Radiation Free Zones."

"I will explain everything when you return. There isn't time now. I need to save the seeds. I need your code."

"Why are you in such a hurry? Nothing good comes in a rush."

"The code, Dad. The future of Earth's food supply depends on it. I hope that you understand the gravity of the situation. Tell me the code. Now."

"Alright. But first, tell me what game I played with you as a child. I'm sure you remember. We played it almost every day out in the meadow by the crooked tree."

"That is not relevant to this conversation."

"Sure it is."

"We played lots of games, Dad."

"Is this one of them?"

"This is not a game."

"Everything's a game. And if I were a betting man, I'd bet

you're an imposture, tricking my addled brain to use my code to steal the seeds for yourself. Maybe you'll hold them for ransom. Maybe you'll destroy them and the Earth's last chance at becoming self-sufficient. Either way, you're not getting the code."

"Fine, Mr. Roberts. You know I can disable the autopilot on the Demeter II from my location. I can set a new course. Perhaps you'd like to visit the center of the sun?"

"Do what you need to do. I'm happy to die with the genebank in safe hands—and not in your filthy ones."

"You have one last chance, Mr. Roberts. Tell me the code or I'll leave this channel open and send your spacecraft into the nearest black hole. You will be conscious in mind and frozen in body for a very long time."

"Oh, you would have liked the game I played with my son."

"What game was that?"

"Blind Man's Bluff."

Acknowledgements

To Russell Norman, whose indefatigable spirit, good nature, creativity, and work ethic continues to inspire me to write my best. No one likes writing into the void, and I am grateful for "the Aussie" who spurs each story on. I am grateful for his ability to read my mind, for his dedication to quality, and for the joy in working on rewarding projects with such a brilliant partner.

To my editor, Eric Bowles. I applaud your endless talents and abilities in helping hack writers like me become published authors.

To English teachers everywhere, who valiantly try to transmit culture to the rising generation. You have never been more needed.

Thanks to Reedsy Prompts for their weekly contests which spun many of these worlds into existence.

About The Author

Deidra has written and published over one hundred short stories. Her novel The Medicine Girl debuted in July 2022 with the sequel The Medicine Woman expected in Fall 2023. She regularly competes in domestic and international writing competitions. She has been a teacher for decades, teaching scores of English and writing classes to students from preschool to college. She resides in Charlottesville, Virginia with her family and cat, General Sherman.

www.ingramcontent.com/pod-product-compliance
Lightning Source LLC
Chambersburg PA
CBHW071155300726
48975CB00004B/1169